1

Dedications

My dedications first start with an apology;

       Forgive me Lord God, my Father for taking so long to start and finish, and yes, everything in your time Father.

To my wife; Chere when only God and you believed more in me and my abilities than I. We are making it off His words alone. God said there were things we had to go through to get this far, the journey is far from over, let's keep praising and growing. Sorry for taking so long to believe you. I love you my Queen.

Ok, this book is dedicated to all the women who inspired me to be a better man than I ever thought I could become.

Devallerie Middleton & Evelyn Roebuck
       R.I.P. Granny & MotherDear

Vicki, Jacki, Eloise, Ann, Mary, Hattie, Kim, Tracy, Rose, Diane and Gloria, Barbara, Lisa, Patricia, Paris, Jennifer, Heather and Chloe.

To my Mom: Vicki, you have been and always
will be a walking, talking, visible Angel in my life.
Thank you for your sacrifice. The Spirit lives
within you. That's what God saved that day.

To all my aunts, if it were not for you ladies I
would have never known what a great woman
looked like and how she should treat a boy who
believes he is a man.

To my sister: Sara Skye, you are the best.
Thanks baby girl for being like my first daughter
and female friend. I love you and continue
conquering the world.

To my daughter: Taryn Olivia, I knew you would
hold my heart well before you came along.
Thank you for the truth you hold in those eyes.

To my son: Nicholas Isaiah, knowing your life
was eminent, inspired me to be a good man so I
could raise a great man. You are the greatest
son a man could ever ask for. Stay yourself.
Thank you my twin.

To all the men in my family thanks for continuing to be good men and great fathers; let's show the world what we are made of......

To all the Mothers & Fathers continue the journey in God's name and your legacies will have everlasting life.

To my brothers: Deon and Darrion our lives inspired this book. Our love for one another continues to be the catalyst for our success.

To my father: Thank you for being my dad.

My story begins in the Dominican Republic, where my father was born. A light brown complected curly haired semi-educated man, my father was a beaucrat whose policies were not well received. My grandfather wanted everyone to receive an education and have opportunities for everyone to succeed, to quote "with everyone's goal being to succeed, our countries can succeed together". His main idea was to unify the Dominican Republic and Haiti, but skin color and language barriers kept this from happening. 'For someone to feel superior they first must make another feel inferior', he would always say. Even though he was 100% Dominican, grandfather was seen as an insurgent- a Haitian sympathizer. He was quickly ousted from his post and sent packing to Haiti with his pregnant wife and their two children. My father was the second of three children and grandfathers' only son. Growing up in Haiti was difficult for my father, he was 10 when he was ousted, and his sister was 13 and despised their father for getting fired and losing the status and comfortable lifestyle in which she was accustomed. The biggest difficulty for my father and his sister was looking different. My father and his sister were Spanish-looking and speaking, and most of the kids in Haiti were African looking and spoke French. Their education exceeded that of the children they were in school with. My father was smart but stayed in trouble, by the time he was 15 he was running the streets, being wild and carefree he liked to say. He loved Haiti. My grandfather had taken ill and wanted my father to be more responsible and become man of the house, but father resisted and grandfather put him out. When we asked Father where he went, he never explained he would only say that he disappeared for those three years.

Now 18, father only came back when his father died; he buried grandfather and convinced his mother to move herself and his sisters back to the Dominican. He stated that there were better opportunities for his sisters and that she could grieve comfortably in a home that he'd found for her and the girls. My father was a con artist, knowing that his mother and eldest sister were nurses', he convinced a doctor he knew that his mother could run his clinic and his sister could assist. The doctor agreed, giving them both positions. They were making at least 3 times more in the Dominican as they did in Haiti. Soon thereafter, the doctor married my father's eldest sister and moved my grandmother and her youngest daughter into his home. My father traveled between Haiti and the Dominican with ease due to his skin color and the officials he knew- or should I say because of the secrets he knew about these officials. On one of these many trips to Haiti he met my mother; he described her as a beautiful cocoa brown goddess, God's greatest gift to him. "My own personal angel", he would always finish with. My mother had the kind of smile that would light up the darkest room, and the kind of spirit that brought happiness and God's joy to anyone who was near. Father made many trips to Haiti, just to see mother until he could convince her to leave and go to the Dominican with him. He got mother a job that the Holiday Resort, as a room attendant, where he also worked as a concierge. Father said foreigners paid more for the services he provided and were more discretionary in their actions. When my mother became pregnant with their first child, Marcelis, the resort fired her and gave father an ultimatum-go back to Haiti with her or send her alone. Mother tried to make the decision for them both: she would leave so that father could keep his job. Father said no and they went back to Haiti, mother and father took odd jobs once they returned and then started working for some prominent officials in Haiti. This went on for a few years and then mother became pregnant with me. They were just making it as it was, but now to be burdened with me made life more than a struggle, we were living in abject squalor. Father received no help from his sister because as she saw it, he'd married a baboon. I was 5 when father decided to go back to the Holiday Resort; he had to start all over working as a cabana boy, this unnerved father. This is when father went back to his old ways of conning and scheming his way into money. He cultivated relationships with the patrons of the establishment, doctors, lawyers, businessmen. He got them drugs, found underground gambling spots, he hustled them as much as he could out of whatever he could. He provided the men with women and unbeknownst to them-their wives with men.

Sometimes, vice versa. He finally convinced this English doctor into bringing us all to England where he would be a butler/caretaker and mother would be a maid and nanny to his children. Off to England we go....

Part II

Father was selling drugs for the doctor, I discovered, even after we got to England his hustling ways continued for the next couple of years. The doctor my father was working for became hooked on the very drugs he was peddling, things started to crumble and since my father was the face of this illegal business all the heat came his way. Police as well as the competition were gunning for him, father was adamant about keeping his family out of harms' way. He arranged for transport on a freighter to the States. Father explained to mother that we would have more freedom and more opportunities in the States, so we gathered what we could and went to the docks, he gave my mother some money and told her to pay this guy for our accommodations and that he would be along shortly, we were at the docks for what felt like days waiting for father to show, until this guy that mother had paid came and said that this was the only window of time for us to board. So we left without my father. We were on a ship headed for God's knows where, sneaking around like the rats we shared containers with, not knowing when we were going to arrive or if we were going to arrive at all. We lived in these containers that were cargo holds for merchandise that was headed for the states. These containers were held in what they call the "bulk" area of the ship, that's the bottom underneath the cabins on the side of the engines, it was cold, dark and wet and smelled of urine and feces, the air was stale and fear was rampant among us. We were not the only stowaways; there were at least 100 of us-mainly women and children. The men that were stowaways, worked as deckhands and cooks to pay their way to the states.

Once we got to the U.S. we began living the American nightmare, segregation-separate but equal. Poverty and ostrasization you name the problem, we faced it, especially homelessness and hunger. The freedom to be homeless and the opportunity to be hungry, I don't think this is what my father had in mind. Being incognito while trying to find employment was very difficult for our mother, going to school and receiving an education was impossible for us, being illegal, not knowing if father was dead or alive was a sore point for us all. Mother tried to keep a positive face, Marcel was sure father had not abandoned us and more than likely was killed by his counterparts or arrested by the police. But I on the other hand, resented my father for putting us in the horrible predicament. Hoping he was dead created a rift between my brother and I but mother tried to keep our spirits high, she would always say "we are all we have". In her words, each other is all we got. That is pretty much what kept my brother and me from tearing into one another. A few months went by with us staying in and out of abandoned buildings or properties, mother finally found a job as a house servant/nanny to a lawyer and his family, it was live-in as they had young children. Which left me and Marcel alone living in a basement of a vacant property. No one knew we were there, we snuck in and out during the night, so we could come and go undetected. We would swipe rations from the local bodegas and local markets, we would leave notes for mother on her room window, so she knew we were ok, this went on for a few months until the family mother worked for went on holiday for 2 weeks. At which time she snuck us into their home; we slept, ate and bathed in this little room they provided her. The lawyer also had a butler who drove and did property repairs, so mother kept us out of his line of sight. He gave mother a little black and white television to watch and help her learn English while the family was gone. She hid it under her bed when the family returned.

Marcel warned me not to steal from this family as mother needed the work and a place to sleep; I guess I had my fathers' penchant for sticky fingers. Although as a hard head, another fraternal trait, I would raid the cupboards and fridge, believing that the food would not be missed. Those 2 weeks were short although magnificent. One evening during this time the butler gave mother $20 to go to the movies to keep her out of the house for a few hours so he could throw a party and no one would be the wiser. But mother knew and did as she was asked; besides she wanted to spend time with us outside of the house and wondered where we slept and ate. It was hard for mother to leave that house as the family depended upon her for everything. Cooking, cleaning, doing laundry and raising their children, the lawyer was always off to work, as for his wife she was always lunching or shopping. The children 5 and 8 forever needed looking after, I grew to hate that family, and mother would always walk them to and from school, wash and bathe them, iron their nice clothes, fix their meals and tell them bed time stories. Marcel saw the anger inside of me boiling, he would always say, 'don't be upset with mother, she's only doing what she must', my rage was not intended for mother but for the rich whites who took the mothers away.

By this time Marcel and I had started running with other Haitian, Dominicans, and Cuban runaways and refugees. We were known as the 'Island Boys'. Neither the black or white Americans liked us very much because we did not understand English or because they could not speak our languages. Stealing most anything we could get our hands on even if the police busted us, we were undocumented kids. We would use American sounding names and say nothing more; they would usually let you go after a few hours depending on your age. Anyone looking over 13 wound up in juvenile detention, those small heists would get you no more than 50-60 bucks, that was good for keeping a couple of bellies full for 2 or 3 days. Then a few of the older guys, tired of small timing it, started selling drugs. The police would usually leave us younger boys in holding, to try and teach us a lesson-it didn't work for those of us who were hungry and were without. Mother held this job at the lawyers' home for just over a year, pretty much leaving me and Marcel orphans. Coming up in the streets of a foreign land forced us to grow up quick; it also made us mentally and emotionally lost. If the fuzz, busted you enough time they shipped you off to Children's services to either get placed in a foster home (usually a white family) or a group home (where you went unnoticed) or you wound up back on the streets. We took to robbing pimps and drug dealers, because those were the only ones with money, where we lived. During one of these incidences, I was stabbed. Marcel had been busted twice for shoplifting; getting revenge on this pimp that stabbed me was his third go-round. It was 3 strikes before California made it legal. They sent him to a group home, after being there for awhile and fighting with some of the boys and staff members he got sent to another state run facility for wayward youths and left me in New York all alone. I tried my best to keep my eye on mother but it got more frustrating to see her being mother to those Caucasian kids.

Besides, we had not contacted mother in about 4 months prior to Mars getting busted so it was no reason to contact her now and worry her with my stabbing and Marcel's arrest. I was trying to prove my worth being a pee wee gangster, I spotted this lowlife pimp smacking one of his lady workers around and taking a couple of bucks from her and add it to this wad of cash he pulled from his pocket. I figured robbing him would make a name for myself, instead of being called Engleberger by the fellas.

I was called this for a few reasons: first, I was the chubby kid of the crew; second, The Bad News Bears was my favorite movie to go see at the local theater (nice place to get out of the cold wet climate New York had to offer) and third, the slight English accent I picked up spending the bulk of my language learning time in England. They called Marcel 'Buckwheat' at first, because of his hair and ratty clothes, after he ripped off a clothing store for a leather jacket and a few pair of jeans they called him Zuco after that Grease character. I just called him Mars, and he called me Baby Bear, I asked him to stop calling me that, it's what our parents called me. Anyway, I was going to catch this pimp off his square, he would not be concerned about a 9 year old kicking a can down the alley where he usually parked his car to watch his girls service their tricks. He was standing in this dark dank alley facing a doorway, I thought he was peeing but to my surprise, this lady was kissing his penis. I hid behind this telephone pole watching in amazement, but then I remembered what I was supposed to be doing, I continued down this dark alley- only the outer street lamps providing what little light they could, I had a wine bottle behind my back wrapped inside a paper bag, I stuck the drinking end into his back and in the deepest voice I could muster I said "Gimme the money!". I guess it did not really spook him like I thought it would, he reached into his coat pocket for what I thought was the money, but he pulled out a switchblade, this all happened so fast, his lady friend jumped up screaming and he'd spun around and jammed the knife into my shoulder (he probably thought he was catching a much taller guy in the gut) before I knew it, he pulled it out and stuck me again, I flung the bottle at his head, the woman pushed him into me and we both fell, him landing on top of me, breaking a couple of ribs in the process. As he looked down at his assailant he said "shit kid, what the hell?" me lying on the ground with a blade broken off in my shoulder, blood squirting, in pain with him running away. Just before I heard his wheels screeching, he said 'fuck!", not hardly able to breathe and tears running, I got to my feet and stumbled out of the alley and finally passed out on the sidewalk moments later, only to come to in the hospital, a victim of a gang fight the nurses tell me.

My predicament and my cute chubby face gets me a lot of attention from the nurses and a lot of ice cream. I spent about a week or more in the hospital, waiting for some caseworker to come get me out of here since I had no known parents. When I first came to after they got the blade out and stitched me up a police officer asked me a lot of questions that I could not answer and many more that I would not answer, to keep Mars and mother out of trouble. I was going to run, but I figured maybe another bed besides the hospital bed for a couple of days would feel real good, but thinking of Mars out there all alone was driving me crazy. After a couple more days in the hospital, I took off only to learn Mars got nabbed for taking a pole to that pimp that stabbed me. One of the pimps' ladies ratted him out to some dirty police officers. They put him on a bus with other kids to Hackensack, NJ, now for the first time I had no one who knew or cared for me. I could go see mother, but what would that solve, like I said we hadn't contacted her in so long, it would just cause more problems. I don't think we realized that our disappearances from her life would rattle her. I learned that mother not knowing our whereabouts made her slack on her job, the lack of attention to her duties got her fired which I did not know, obviously she could not officially look for us. She wound up staying with a day maid that she had made friends with. When I went to look in on her, I found some maids who knew of her and I was told of her situation. I did my best to keep tabs on mother, but I had to do what mother tasked of me and Mars-no matter what, stay together. Couple of the other island boys and I hopped a train and off to Jersey we go, the eldest of us was 14 year old Dominic aka "Ghost", I later found out his twin sister was the prostitute in the alley that night. Because he knew how *everything* went down, and I don't remember him being with me in that alley that night.

The other 2 tagalongs on that journey were 11 year old, Essien aka "Baby" and 12 year old Paulo aka "Epstein", I was the youngest but I was also the biggest. Ghost was ok with leaving his sister Dominique back in New York because Mars beat that Puerto Rican pimp half to death with that pole, when she cut out of that alley she ran to an all girl halfway house and hid out there, scared to death that her pimp had killed me. Ghost told me the story as we rode to Jersey to get Mars out of the detention center, we had no idea how we were going to do just that, but I was responsible for Mars being jammed up, so it was my responsibility to get him out. Mars became the leader of our pack even though he was only 11, he was the boldest, craziest and smartest of us all, and he was also the most daring of any of the Island boys. Mars kept us fed and in warm places, he kept us out of the sight of police and children services. Dominic was the eldest of us all, he passed for the white kid, so the shop owners followed us around the store while he boosted anything he could, usually bologna, cheese, chips, anything edible. Every once in a while we got something hot to eat. Hot dogs, polishes usually something that we could boil or pan fry, most any other hot meals were pizza slices or burgers. But that was only when we got a big score of $100 or more, which was rare. The Island boys crew were twelve strong at one point, but lack of direction and strong leadership had the boys leaving, they had to strike out on their own just to make it on these streets. Some of the guys got busted, some got killed and others either started selling drugs, using them or selling their bodies. Most kids in our situation get strung out on drugs or start selling them to anyone who would buy. Heroin and marijuana mainly, but some of them could get their hands on PCP, LSD or cocaine. We weren't dealers, but if we robbed one and happened to get what he was carrying, we weren't afraid to sell it just to feed ourselves. It was only 4 of us left from the original crew. There were a couple of guys that left but would come around from time to time because we were the only family they really knew, that was Natine who we called "Chuy" and Ignacio who we called "El Jefe" he hated that name-he called himself Nacho because he always had money. He would spend yours and keep his for himself. Ignacio was our original leader, but I figured being responsible for more than just himself was too much to bear, we figured that was also his main reason for taking off, El Jefe wasn't the type to share and he didn't see himself as a boss, that's why he hated the nickname 'El Jefe'.

He was 16, had been on the streets of New York for three years, he was a Cuban guy who came from Miami in the back of a truck to work for some Colombian cat who thought he was going to become king of New York. Jefe said this guy was bad news, he bought kids over from Cuba on promises of wealth and freedom, but had them selling and trafficking his drugs from Florida. All over the East coast, Jefe said that this guy kept a tight reign over the kids and that he only gave them enough money to eat with. He owned a building that should have been condemned but it's where he kept everyone who worked for him. I asked Jefe how many kids were working for this guy; he said he didn't know, that the numbers always changed and that if you didn't do what you were told that you would be tortured. Whenever Jefe would talk about his time working for the Columbian he would drift off into deep thought, when he finally came to his eyes were watery and his body would be shaking. He would only want to laugh and not talk anymore; he usually took off and went to the movies or wound up watching cartoons on the television and zoning out. I gather most of us have seen or maybe even done some things out on these streets that would make us zone out too, no need to bore you with stories about us all. Most of the kids we met out here were in some way, shape or form of African descent even though we came from different places; Cubans, Haitians, Dominicans and Jamaicans, we all spoke similar languages and had similar dreams. I didn't

notice the similarities until later on in my life,
back then the only similarities were the need for
food, shelter and family structure. We could
help one another provide 2 of the 3 but without
the third it was useless, a bunch of kids trying to
be adults in a foreign place. Without
supervision, structure or money, besides the
scars of our travels and homelands ran deep and
wide, kept us from really gelling like we
could've; we stayed mainly in 2 areas of New
York, the Bronx and Queens, even though the
transit system being so vast we traveled all over
the city getting into all kinds of trouble.
Brooklyn was a great place to hang, but the
American blacks kept a tight hold onto their
neighborhoods and we were seen as just darker
Spanish people and there was a race war going

on among everyone. It's going on everywhere at all times. Whites or lighter skins blacks put all their problems, hate and dishonor on those of us that are dark or a darker hue, let the hate fit the difference. The ruling class usually used any difference to push their agenda or just to feel superior than they actually are. The train ride to Jersey seemed like it went on forever, even though it was just a couple of hours. After Ghost told us what went down with Mars, the car was quiet-or at least the inside of the jalopy. This car rattled more than a room full of babies, but I guess beggars can't really be choosers. When we got to Jersey we had to make connections with some of the street kids just to find out where the juvie home was. At first, we figured that one of us would get into some kind of trouble for doing what we do, but we could not be sure that this would get us sent to the same place Mars was sent. The only option we were left with was to hold up and set up shop in Jersey until our goal was accomplished, as you can imagine, this plan took time. Jersey was way different than New York; it was open season in Jersey, just a couple more problems we had to overcome. One, most everyone was poor or it seemed that way, two, cops were way more dirty three, the cops were way more racist as well. In New York, it was one and a half to every five cops you would have a problem with, here it was more like 3 to 5 times more likely that if you got pinched they not only robbed you they kicked your ass for good measure. But hate is pretty much the same everywhere, we always thought the Bronx was bad but Jersey was on a whole other level. Not realizing until later on that we made our way through Newark, it was the port of call for the ship we were on, once the ship docked we were hold up there for a few days until things calmed down and the docks were emptied, mainly late nights to early mornings. Then we were hustled off the ship into a waiting van that took us to our final stop in New York City. Since it was daytime everything seemed normal, as the evening drew near I started to panic, where would we sleep? Where would we eat? How long will this last? Just seeing Newark brought back a flood of memories about that time on the ship.

Sleeping in the containers aboard the ship, I thought everyone on the ship were stowaways like us. The fact that it was mainly women and children left the females vulnerable to attack as we had seen and heard on several occasions. Mars decided that we could sleep at the entrance of the container so any of the bad men trying to get at the mothers and sisters, would have to step over one of us or trip over us all and once he fell-we would attack, cutting and stabbing him with knives we stole from the kitchen and other objects that could be used as weapons that we found in the containers. We lay in twos about a foot and half apart staggered for security purposes. Marcel and I had witnessed a women being attacked, she was pulled into a storage room by two men-they punched and slapped her and tore the clothes from her body. As one guy ripped at her clothes the other man a skinny dirty man who always smelled horrible was pulling his pants down, he grabbed her neck and screamed for her to open her mouth, at first she would not so he slapped her harder, making her bleed from the nose. The other man, a large equally smelly bloke just laughed as he undressed breathing heavily saying all the while 'yeah, get her'. Through all this confusion, she sees us standing there, the skinny man notices she is looking at something, he turns around and sees us and I scream out "mother!" the woman screams "my children!" the skinny man grabs at his pants down around his ankles and tries to run, he falls into the fat man, they get up and finally gather themselves and run past us-the woman grabs at me and rushes us in the other direction. When she stops running I see her crying and shaking, she hugs us and tells us 'protect your mother', that was one of many attacks aboard the ship.

Mother had us hum some native songs and some new American songs to keep us from crying and realizing our predicament, we walked and hummed through the streets of New York, no direction would solve our problems-now that is truly being lost. When turning in either direction yields no answer, how can I not cry when mothers eyes welled up with water at the thought of what is she supposed to do? Seeing our mother in that kind of distress broke our hearts, it is probably the main reason Mars and I stayed away from mother, believing that without us to feed, clothe and shelter she would be better off. We were ignorant in our beliefs because we needed each other equally.

The guys and I were in Jersey for about a month trying to put up some cash, whatever we stole, jacked or snatched, if it was cash we put away half to make sure once we had Mars we had enough for shelter and food for all of us. We would steal jewelry and sell it to a dealer for money or trade it for drugs which we would turn around and sell to a junkie for cash. It was slow going, being new faces made everybody pay extra special attention to us so instead of sticking people up in the streets, it was easier to follow them home and case the place. We'd wait until they left-our motto was to 'never walk out with more than your pockets could hold.' A lot of people would leave their windows open or their doors unlocked; we'd sneak in and go through drawers, check under beds and mattresses. Our weekly haul was about $300 bucks, at first, we stayed a week at the Sleepy Bear motel, and everybody thought it was good luck, seeing how Mars always called me "Baby Bear We just showed up with another family and confused the desk clerk, Ghost passed for a white boy, so no one ever questioned him; besides when you pay for a whole week with cash, rarely are there any questions. Two to a bed and bologna and chips were on the menu. We stole a car to get around and we hid it behind the motel to keep it from being found. We snuck out the bathroom window and drove into the more seedy parts of Hackensack. When you are out hustling, eyes and ears are usually on high alert. But that also means mouths are running like faucets, because it's the only thing that makes time go by. Making money the way we did we made friends quick- but made enemies even quicker, Ghost and I finally found a place for us to crash so we can stay in the thick of things. Coming and going was too suspicious, if the streets don't see you all day they don't want to know you at night. It was going on about six weeks since I had seen or even talked to Mars. But the information we got was good, we got numbers to a few boys homes and addresses as well, I hoped to God Mars was using his American name, because that was the only way we could find him. During the day we would post up on the corner across the street from one of the homes or at least a couple of blocks away depending on the area, maybe we'd catch a glimpse of him. We would use the payphone to call the home and in as much as we could muster an authoritative voice we'd ask if they had a Marcel Langley residing in the facility. Your words had to be very adult-like (educated) and short and to the point or you would get nowhere fast. If we messed up and said the wrong thing or used the wrong words we would have to wait a couple days to call back, time enough for the counselors to forget. We finally got a break that Mars was sent to a new facility in Trenton for psychiatric treatment- a place called St. Charles. Ep said that he was sent there for his ongoing involvement in altercations with facility staff and residents. That explained nothing. That left us all confused as we kept asking around trying to find out what happened with Mars, we didn't bother to find out where this St. Charles place was or even Trenton for that matter. Epstein had talked with some of the kids at this home in Hackensack, he spoke Spanish fluently along with Baby, but Ghost and I could only understand a little. So it was up to Baby and Ep to get the skinny on Mars. He was placed there because he spoke Spanish as well, Spanish was fathers' natural tongue, mothers' was French, which I spoke and Ghost as well. We all spoke broken English, more slang than actual English because most of the boys here spoke Spanish and were undocumented, this was their destination.

Epstein and Baby were told that some of the older kids picked on Mars, stole his clothes, food and whatever else they could get their hands on. Mars in turn would fight these boys and recruit other younger boys that were being bullied to gang up on the older ones. Until they stopped picking on the others and concentrated on Mars, that only made Mars angrier, so he got hold of two knives while on dish duty and attacked a few of the boys in their sleep. So they shipped him off to the mental hospital in Trenton, New Jersey. This is another reason we wound up on the streets of Jersey for longer than anticipated. We found out Trenton was an hour and a half to 2 hours south of Hackensack, Mars was either in Trenton or he could have been transferred to a facility in Philadelphia, depending on the doctor's assessment. It was either my guilt, love or fear for Mars that ran deep, because this was getting monotonous but as Ghost put it-what else we got to do? By the time we took off for Trenton or Philly, we saved up about $900, would have been more but information costs like everything else in America, but to four kids in a stolen car it might as well have been a million dollars. All the contacts, living life in the street and gaining street skills would all come in handy in my later years.

We all had dreams. America was to be our salvation. The land of milk and honey, the home of many opportunities, a place where a poor man could realize his dreams. For those of us who could not pass as white or at least be light enough to be excused, this dream was a joke. These feelings are becoming all too familiar; persecution, classism, racism or just plain old hate. We could've stayed in England or, for that matter my family could have remained in Haiti. For most of the 70's, the Dominican Republic was off limits to us darkies. I guess nowhere on God's green Earth was there a safe haven. Ghost put the radio on to deaden the silence, we drove at night, less police on the road and Ghost could pass as just another white teenager heading anywhere in his car. The rest of us kept low and sang along to the tunes that were playing just to keep Ghost from falling asleep. Baby and Ep had given this Puerto Rican lady $100 to find out as much as she could about Mars; she gave them her telephone number so we could call from time to time in case any more information had become available. No matter where we wound up Trenton or Philly we would have to start this search and rescue process all over. Right outside of Trenton we stopped and found a ratty motel that we could get a little shut eye, wash our face and hands and get a bite to eat. In the morning, we would call the Puerto Rican woman to see if she had an exact destination for us. This motel room was filthy just as bad as the abandoned buildings we slept in back in New York- had more roaches though. I couldn't sleep or do much of anything else so I opened the curtain a little just to have something to stare at, the little black and white TV the room had didn't work even though back in those days at that time of morning only thing on would either be snow or the American national anthem. The room only had one full size bed, which was tattered and stained, I believe it was just a couple of pieces of foam with a fitted sheet around them to keep them together, but anything softer than the ground was a welcomed change. Ghost and Ep shared the bed and baby piled our coats onto the desk as a make shift bed and pillow. Ghost and Ep went to sleep as soon as their heads hit the mattress. Baby and I talked a little until he finally drifted off; I believe it was four o'clock in the morning. I sat in this dirty ass chair and daydreamed about a better life and my family back together. Once I was sure that the guys were deep into their sleep I cried a silent cry, staring into the darkness, the only light being that of the red dimmed light bulbs on the vacancy sign of this cheap motel. The tears tracing my dirty face as they ran from my eyes, I couldn't cry while the others were woke, no signs of weakness, fear or sadness or it would destroy us. I felt like the big brother to these three guys even though I was the youngest. The sun was rising and I walked over to the bathroom and peed then washed my face and hands. Baby tossed and turned all night that desk must not have been as comfortable as he thought. All the coats were on the floor I shook them out and searched the pockets for the number of the Puerto Rican woman. Once I had the number I left the room and went to the payphone that was at the end of the hallway on the wall. I called her to see if she had any more information, but there was no answer, maybe she wasn't home. I called three more times before I headed back to the room. It was about 11 o'clock. The guys were woke and hungry so we walked around the corner to this greasy spoon to get something to eat, we all had some griddle cakes, bacon and milk. After eating we were left sitting on our hands. Baby and Ep wanted to go see a movie so that's what we did just to kill some time. To this very day I couldn't tell you what we saw because the only thing that was on my mind was Mars and how he was doing. I guess this is how mother constantly feels. When we get back we must visit mother and let her know how we are faring.

After the movies we drove into Trenton parked

and walked around, taking in the surroundings, trying to find out where kids in our situation would hang out, wind up or find themselves. It's not as difficult as you would think, any strange looks from the people on the streets is a good sign of whether or not you belonged. Trenton was a hard place to discern seeing as everywhere we went was both ghetto and working class. I found a payphone and made another call to the PR woman, still no answer, I was getting angry and more frustrated. Were we here by mistake? Could Mars be back in New York, Hackensack or some place all together different? With all this being unknown I was even more scared and lost than I was when we first set foot in America. Oh well, we must keep trudging on.

MARS

When mother finally got the job with this lawyer in his home Bear and I had to go it alone, I was in charge and responsible for our well being. For the first few weeks it was tough, we had to be without mother's guidance and nurturing spirit, but we do what we must. Bear was distraught and he cried a lot at first so I screamed for him to stop crying, shut up and grow up and get over it. I might have been a little hard on him, hitting and scratching him and sometimes I would choke him. The constant crying and whining were unbearable. I guess anger was my way of dealing with what was happening to my family. Bear never said a word to mother about how I treated him and mother never asked. Until one time we went to see mother and bear had a scar on his neck from where I scratched, the wound was deep and long and was very noticeable, Bear could never lie to mother, so he began telling mother of all I had done. Mother was angry and she grabbed me up and said that this was her child and you will not put your hands on him and that if I ever harmed him again she would break my little neck. At the time I believed her threats of breaking my neck and I also believed that Bear was more important and that she loved him more than she loved me. Mother told me that I was the oldest and that Bear looked up to me like I was a superhero. She said that Bear loves me and it would be disrespectful of me to destroy our brotherly bond. I did not believe her. As I reflect on the past mother was right as usual. But being responsible for not only myself but a whiny child made me very angry and bitter this rage blinded me of my own guilt. Our last time seeing mother was when the lawyer took his family on holiday, we spent two weeks at their home in a tiny bedroom that was provided to mother, we were not suppose to leave this room for any reason for fear of being spotted by the only other person in the house, the butler, he kept an eagle eye on mother. Bear, being a spoiled baby did as he pleased and almost got caught on a couple of occasions- mother said nothing. When the visit was over and this family came back I no longer wanted to visit mother again, I am not sure if it was the trouble I got in for beating up Bear or if was seeing how this family lived and Bear and I barely had food to eat. I wanted that life, so I set out to get it by any means. This is when Bear and I hooked up with other kids in our situation, we called ourselves The Island Boys, we had a few girls but it was more boys so hence the name. We stole everything we could get our hands on and would sell any merchandise that we couldn't use ourselves.

The big things at that time was selling dope, pimping women and stick-ups, I guess nothing has really changed. The island boys mainly did stick-ups- we targeted the dealers and their customers, took any cash and the drugs they had, turned around and sold the dope we stole for more cash. We ran in stores and boosted clothes, jewelry and electronics. Life was hard, when you could sleep it was usually on a hard floor in some busted up building eating what you could find in trash cans or steal from local markets. Most of the time I stayed woke just to keep us safe. I started drinking to take the pain away and that led to smoking marijuana which kept me hungry, so we robbed more bodegas and fruit stands it was a vicious cycle but it kept us alive. I tried my best to keep Bear away from drinking and the dope but I couldn't stop the others or myself for that matter. One of the older guys who used to run with our crew was selling drugs full-time no more boosting and penny ante schemes for him he said; now he always had money, a place to stay and never ate from the garbage. My first thought was this is the route I need to take. My first night out on the block was kind of scary, I told Bear and the other guys that I was headed out to scout potential places to rob and maybe I could come up on a couple bucks to put in our savings can, my father always said "have enough for later on" and that there is always a later on, even if it's not one for you.

The junkies looked very similar to zombies. They didn't care who they copped from as long as they were getting their fix it didn't matter, that's how come so many of them got taken. They walked through the night with careless abandon. What scared me the most was not the night zombies or possibly being killed in the street over drugs, but how I visualized them and the situation, all I saw was potential....my potential victims, my means to wealth. I could rob, steal or even kill without remorse. I was so good at what I was doing that

I could tell who was going to pay cash or who was going to pay in trade from a block away. Even after they bought the dope I was still contemplating robbing them for the rest of their cash and taking what I sold them back to get the next sucker. That night was my foray into drinking and smoking in excess. My thoughts terrified me and this was the only thing that kept me from thinking all together. My other big fear was that Bear would become just like me. Everything we were doing was without provocation. Oh, there were plenty of reasons and concerns and I guess those were just enough to keep us doing what we thought we needed to do. To make the kind of money we needed I figured I would have to be out on the block like a prostitute. But that would leave Bear pretty much alone and he was no one else's problem.

I was on the block selling my dope when Bear was stabbed. Ghost was looking for me to tell me what had happened, it was a few hours before he could find me. I was in another area of the city; this is the area the Island boys stayed out of because it was run by several other gangs that did not take to anyone poaching on their territory. Dealing in this area kept Bear and the others from knowing what I was doing, but dealing here was better than sharing floors with junkies and rats, it was the same place and same smell just a different hell. By the time Ghost found me we figured Bear was in the hospital or already dead. All I could remember was that the last time I saw him I was drunk and high and screaming that he was to blame for our circumstances, we wouldn't even be here if he was never born. We argued back and forth and he was just trying to keep from crying. I was his big brother and here I am blaming him for everything. I am his only connection to love, I miss my baby brother. At the time, thinking through the haze of alcohol and marijuana none of that mattered. We just kept arguing until we started to fight, well, more like wrestle we were rolling around until I ended up on top choking him, the guys were trying to pull me off him then he punched me in my nose and I started to bleed which made me even angrier and go at him harder. When they finally got us apart Bear was bleeding and crying and I was bleeding and cursing at him, I ran from the building and just stayed away. Not being around the guys fueled my drinking and smoking, it was non-stop. Drunk and high is how I wanted to stay, I never realized that in that state of mind I was angrier and more violent than before. When Ghost caught up with me and explained how Bear was out taking up the slack that I left behind and keeping the crew together, putting money up, keeping food in bellies and providing them with a warm safe place to sleep then I realized what I meant to the crew and what the drinking and drugs had done to me. That was just like Bear I thought, not to even need me. He was a watcher, he noticed and heard everything all while staying incognito; we should have called him Ghost or the Invisible man. Ghost told me that his twin sister's pimp stabbed Bear; she told him that Bear was trying to rob the pimp, so that piece of shit stabbed my brother over a few dollars. Not seeing our own culpabilities showed our adolescence, Bear should have never been in that alley as I sit and think more rational, we should never have been in that situation at all. Not just me and bear but the thousands of kids just like us. I now know that this is just life.

I was enraged going back to the thoughts of how mother was attacked on that ship feelings of helplessness poured over me then but not this time, I can do something more about this situation. Remembering how my mother fought and struggled with those men, watching them slap, punch and beat mother taking off their clothes and tearing at hers, frozen in fear and locked in confusion, tears streaming down my face unable to breathe, hoping and praying that it would stop, wondering where my father was and how he had put us in this trouble and how come no one was helping. All I could see was mothers cries for helps and her pleas for them to stop, then I hear Bear scream out, then mother screamed, the men pushed by me and Bear knocking us down, mother ran to us, picked us both up at the same time and we went back to the containers. For the next few days mother would not leave the containers, I figured the weeks we spent on that ship changed me forever. I no longer was a child and would never be able to trust men, especially white men; I couldn't believe Bear could be so absent minded at the time but as I know now we cope with pain and anger in different ways. The trauma of watching your mother raped or any woman, for that matter, can cut deep leaving scars on your soul. I resented Bear a lot for how he internalized everything, it would seem as though nothing even mattered or bothered him. Most of the crew members aboard that ship were oblivious to our presence, but the few who were aware, went into two categories: foe or enemy. One of the men who knew of our presence was a cooks' assistant, and he took a shine to Bear, so he would always give Bear treats, which Bear would share with me and some of the other children. After the incident with mother I came up with a plan to keep us safe: we would move the mothers and sisters to the back of the containers and the sons would sleep in two staggered from the front to the back, with the older boys in the front and some in the middle as guards. Bear got several knives from the kitchen, some of the other children and I found other items that we could use as weapons, most of the knives went to the women; we kept two- one at the front and one in the middle. My solution worked well. When those two problems came looking for trouble, they found more than they bargained for, after that night my mother left the container, she never stopped carrying that knife. The crew members who knew of our existence ceased their raids on all the containers for fear of disappearing like the other two. Even the cooks' assistant stopped showing favor. The next few days went by mostly uneventful, listen to me ramble on, those memories are the reason I'm here.

After Ghost told me that this pimp named El Guapo stabbed Bear and took off I could barely think straight, I just took off and left my post which would get me in trouble. I went looking for this El Guapo, it took a couple of days because he was lying low, and he thought he killed this kid he stuck. I found him a few nights later, I followed him as he collected from his hoes, then went to cop for his habit figuring he was headed someplace to get fixed, I thought this was my chance. Not only to get revenge for what he did to Bear but also to rip him off, 3 days worth of hoe money should net me a tiny profit, especially since it was a Monday night after the weekend. I figured I would have enough to buy my own stash of dope and be my own boss. I grabbed up this pipe I saw in the alley and followed him back to his hideout. He went up the back stairs of this apartment building to the second floor. I climbed the fire escape to sit and wait; I saw my chance when this white guy came to the building using the same back entrance. I knew this building; this is where Ghosts' auntie lived. His aunt was a junkie I knew because she was one of my customers and Guapo's bottom girl. I went in through a hall window and heard the white guy and Guapo talking and laughing. I went back to the fire escape to look through the window; the white guy went into another room with Ghosts' aunt. I thought it was just a john and I went back to the front door and knocked.

Guapo must have been high as a kite because he didn't ask who it was, he just opened the door, I stood to the right of the door and readied my swing, he said 'come on in' and stumbled back to the couch, where he sat with dazed eyes and a slight grin on his face. I just started swinging this pipe for all I was worth, the next thing I knew this white guy comes out of this room in just his drawers and a shirt and tackles me to the floor. He puts a gun to my head, the auntie is screaming, he is screaming, my eyes are bulging out because I believe this is it, the white man is about to blow me away and all I could see was my mother, father, Bear and I, the way we were back in Haiti. Then I hear the white guy scream to the auntie 'go get my shit bitch!' She leaves and comes back with his clothes.

This white guy is a cop, a detective; he handcuffs me and tells me to stay on the floor while he gets dressed. All the blood in Guapo's battered body sobers them both up quick, auntie is nervously pacing and the cop tells her to stop but I don't think she can. He says let me think almost a hundred times and then he starts screaming at me, asking 'what the hell did you do kid?' and why did I do this? All the while I just kept looking over at Guapo hoping that as hard and as many times as I hit him with that pipe, his nasty, filthy ass was dead. Auntie dropped to her knees trying to get Guapo to get up, she reaches over to the phone to try and get help, and I guess she wasn't that sober, cause the police was already there, with his foot in my back. He rushes over to where she is and knocks her away from the phone; kind of too late she already gave her address. This cop started grabbing dope and money off the table and floor; he runs to the door and looks back as if to survey the room making sure he has everything, he pauses and still sees me lying on the floor, cuffed, he says "shit!" I guess he wasn't sober either; he couldn't leave me there for some other cops to find. He stuffed the money and dope in his pockets and put his jacket on. Smiling and thinking to myself, he almost left me here. I looked back over to Guapo, who by only some twist of cruel fate is moving and trying to get up. The cop snatches me to my feet and we run out of the building, he shoves me into his car and we take off. He drives around for about 10 minutes and then he finally pulls over, he bangs on the steering wheel saying over and over "fuck! Shit!" he reaches into his pocket, pulls out some dope, and sniffs it up. I'm thinking to myself-he's going to kill me, was I imagining things or was Guapo still alive? This junkie ass cop is going to kill me and leave me dead in the alley, we sat in his car for what felt like hours, and then he reaches into his pocket and pulls out the money-my money and starts counting. We're both startled by a knock at his window, it's a uniformed officer, he puts the window down and the uni asked if everything is ok, the detective showed the uni his badge and then hands the uni $100 of what was supposed to have been my money and asked the uni to run me in for possession. The uni then asked 'where's the dope?' the detective then hands him a bag of what he was snorting just minutes ago. The uni opens the back door and snatches me out of the detectives' car, at that moment I thank God- it was the first time I spoke to God since we got on that ship. Well, thanks God-I guess. I kept my mouth shut through this whole ordeal, the uni put me in the back of his squad car. Staying quiet was our norm, it was better to have big ears than a big mouth. The uniformed cop drove a few blocks and picked up his partner from this local spot that was well known as "The Color Barrier", it's where white cops kept their minority girlfriends, knowing that their wives and girlfriends would never venture into this part of town to verify any suspicious activity that their men might be up to. It's funny how some of the big time gangsters had the same idea and sometimes even the same chick. I guess that's why cops and criminals hated each other so much, they were only separated by time and expectation. After his partner got in the car, I figured they would pocket the dope and money and let me go-not the case. They ran me in and booked me for loitering. It was late, no child service workers were available, and so they took me straight to a halfway house to hold me overnight seeing as the only thing I would say was "no comprende" to all of their questions and couldn't give them a phone number or an address of a parent or guardian.

I wound up in this detention center not too far from where the uni picked his partner up from, after I was checked in, they told me to shower and gave me some clothes and a cot to sleep on. Told me to get some sleep because wake up time was in a few hours and I could get something to eat and a counselor would be around to talk to me. I lay down on this cot, trying to replay the events of the night in my head. I couldn't remember for the life of me what got me here. I fell asleep, slept real hard until someone came to wake us, this room was filled with boys just like me-some my age, some older and younger. Most of these boys resembled me color wise, but as I saw it they were all enemies to me. As I moved along through this facility, I watched and listened as hard as I could, watching is a good source of information but listening is an even better source. They hustled us from the bunk room to the bathroom and then to a cafeteria-what they called a mess hall. After I got my tray with a bowl of gray glop, hard bread and two pieces of light brown sticks that was supposed to be sausage, I could see why they called it mess, but I was hungry, so suffice it to say that mess was good. After breakfast, they hustled us back to the bunk room where we waited to be seen by a counselor, being one of the new guys all eyes were on me. Everyone was sizing you up. I tried to keep a gas face on to keep from becoming a target, mentally swimming through all of the events and what I was going to say to the counselor. I remembered Bear and how I was going to kick his butt for getting me locked up. Then it dawned on me that Bear was stabbed and I didn't even bother to find out whether or not he was ok or even alive, Ghost didn't tell me or couldn't tell me of Bear's whereabouts or his wellbeing or maybe he did and I couldn't remember. The more I thought about Bear and what happened to him the more emotional I got. I started to tear up, then when I thought about telling mother that Bear was dead and it was my fault for drinking and doing drugs and I was out selling dope when Bear was stabbed to death. Trying to get money to take care of the others and himself because we fought and I left. The watery eyes moved to a full on cry. The other boys saw me crying and that was not good but I could not stop, I tried to hide my tears and emotions, but it was impossible. These feeling were overwhelming, which made the tears flow unyieldingly. Finally one of the guards came and got me and several others to go talk to a counselor. For me it was too late, I was going to be labeled a cry baby and an easy mark for bullying. As the 5 of us walked to the front of the facility, I felt all eyes on me-I was doomed. When it came time for me to talk with the counselor I kept it real simple: my parents are both dead; my mom died during child birth and my father became a junkie and died of an overdose. I was raised by my mother's sister who was a junkie prostitute, been on the streets since I was 4 or 5, don't really know my birthday. Never had a party or nothing to celebrate my birth so it would come and go with me not knowing. It was a female counselor so my story pulled at her heart strings, she couldn't find out about my mother or Bear. Then the police would go looking for them and we'd all get shipped back to Haiti. The bad part about that is we'd get shipped separately. The tears I shed were real because I didn't know if Bear was dead or alive. Although she felt sorry for me, my story revealed that there was no one to take care of me. So just maybe the facility would provide me shelter, food and education until I was found a foster home. I was stuck here. They sent me back to my bunk, on that long walk back, I heard all kinds of taunts 'baby want a bottle, baby need his mommy, baby needs his blanky' and the name calling was worse, cry baby, little punk, sissy, fag even waterworks-if you can think of it, I was called it. I was picked on mercilessly, I was the chief target of the older boys' ire, but it was not limited to me alone.

Most of the younger boys who were not known to or protected by the older boys were targets as well. It was a nightmare, they would take your food, piss on your clothes, make you do their schoolwork and house chores and when they felt the need to hit something or someone you didn't want to be in their sights. It seemed as if I was always in someone's sight. I tried to fight as best as I could, but they would rat pack you in the shower, bathrooms, hallways or anywhere they could. If you told the guards or counselors that and get them in trouble, the beatings and hazing got worse. I learned that the hard way. Until one day I got fed up with this tortuous treatment which went on for weeks. I got a bunch of the boys who were also punching bags, we would always be seen together we would find or fashion weapons out of anything we could find. We also went on attack raids of our own. Catching one or two of the older boys and whooping on them. Stealing clothes, pushing their meal trays on the floor, spitting in their food, pissing on them in the middle of the night. This was very effective. Finally we had a semblance of peace. Our crew was big, bad and untouchable; we got to all the newcomers first and offered protection. Most of them would turn us down at first but after a few day of treatment they came begging for help. After a while, we little guys outnumbered the big guys. Unfortunately, we had infiltrators acting as victims; some protected boys were acting and promising our members protection if they switched sides. Since they were more scared of the older and bigger guys' retribution, it was scarier than anything we could do. The crew started dwindling until the crew was just me. They figured since I was the one amassing a counteroffensive against them, they would take away my protection, but when I realized that something was wrong inside the crew I knew that it was only a matter of time before I was alone so while they were busy collecting numbers, I got busy collecting weapons. I allowed the older boys to believe I was weak and scared. My strategy was to make them believe they had won. This would lull them into a false bravado and sense of security. To make this plan take effect I had to take a couple more whooping and get myself sent to the infirmary. The infirmary was where I had my cache of weapons; my plan was in full effect by this time. They thought they had won. It was my turn; the nurse said I got whooped so bad that I would need to be on bed rest for at least a week. I had two black eyes, busted ribs, swollen lips and quite a few knots or war wounds on my head, but those weren't deterrence's, those bruises were my spoils of victory. I wasted no time, immediately I went on the attack. The first night in the infirmary, I got my weapons of choice and started with the biggest and oldest of my assailants, cutting and stabbing their arms, legs, ankles and hands-immobilizing them. I put my enemies inside with me. I could torture them anytime or as much as I wanted. I would hold onto my meds so I could double them up, keep them drowsy and sleepy so they were unaware of my movements, after the big guys were gone I went for the infiltrators. I would beat them with socks filled with oranges and apples. My attacks went on for a week before I was caught. The nurse was changing my linen and found some of my arsenal, she informed the guards to pay special attention to me. She figured I was protecting myself but when the guard followed me to the bunkroom he saw me about to pounce on another one of my victims. Thinking that they were ambushing me, I attacked him and another guard. They placed me into a room all by myself and in the morning sent me to see a therapist, between me not knowing if Bear was alive or dead and what happened to me in that detention center, anger and mistrust were taking over.

I refused to talk to anyone; the therapist said that I had severe depression, retardation along with some other problems.   He shipped me off to an actual doctor, a psychiatrist who could better diagnose me, I was sent to a hospital in Trenton, NJ that specialized in child psychology. Once there they would watch me for a couple of days, I would not interact with the other children, I refused to do what the nurses' and attendants asked of me, I was no more than an animal in their zoo- a lab rat for their medication. I was so angry about everything in my life that I lashed out at anything and anyone, especially the doctor they made me see. He diagnosed me with strong violent tendencies, aversion to authority figures, depression, anger and other mental defects.

Then he called me a psychopathic threat to society. After 2 weeks there, I was once again shipped off to another medical facility in Philadelphia, where I was stamped criminally insane. I hate America and everything it stands for. Here I sit in my own mess trying to kick the medication they shove down your throat. Trying to stop from getting electrocuted into normalcy, the thought of my family is the only thing that keeps me from succumbing to complete and utter madness.

GHOST

I was feeling lost, even more now than I ever have, the only family I loved was falling apart Zuco, Bear and the rest of the fellas are like brothers. With Zuco and Bear fighting and arguing more and more it's becoming very clear to me that I have to move on before they leave me like everyone else.

I have a twin sister that only Zuco knows about, some things you have to keep to yourself, one time when Zuco and I were out on a stake out in Brooklyn we ran into Dominique, she told us that she was looking for our Aunt Regine. When Dominique and I came to New York City from Louisiana we were only 9 yrs. old and Aunt Regine was going to be our guardian now. Moving away from the only home we knew was scary for us, especially moving to a big city like New York, it was strange but exciting, we figured that everything was going to be great living with our Mother's sister; we were going to be a family once again. Our Mother passed away when we were just 5; Aunt Regine said it was cancer. We grew up in the Bayou, Mother was a high yellow negro woman, that's how she described herself, Mother would never tell us who our father was so when she died we got passed on to her boy friend at the time, Chuckie, he was a shrimper, he left us with his Mother "Momma Syracuse". She was this old Racist white lady who never treated us with respect and was never nice. Our mother always told us to be proud black people, she said "Our daddy was a white man but that our granddaddy was black and that's the way the rest of the world would always see us, so that's why you should always be proud black people cuz her daddy was".

My momma dying was the saddest day of my life.

We went to live with Momma Syracuse, Chuckie and their family, there were four other kids in the house besides me and Dominique, they were older and we didn't know if they were related to Momma Syracuse and Chuckie but they were white, so they got treated better than us even though we could pass. Momma Syracuse never called us by name like she did with the other children. She called us 'nigga boy' or 'nigga girl'. Chuckie knew we hated it there, but there was no place else for us to go.

He knew our mother had a sister but didn't know where she lived only that her name was Gine. He promised me and Dominique that he would find her and see if she would take us then we could go and live with her. Here we were with Momma Syracuse in the Bayou for 4 years then one day while Momma Syracuse was out Chuckie came home and threw some of our clothes in a sack and took us to the city gave us $50 in an envelope with a note and Aunt Regine's address, put us on a bus and told us to never come back. When we finally got off that bus we were in New York City, it was like a dream, all the big buildings all the people walking all over the place. Gine picked us up from the bus station and took us back to her place. When we got to her place she said "welcome to Harlem" it was a two bedroom apartment Dominique got her own room and Gine told me that the couch was my new bed, any place far from Momma Syracuse was heaven to me. We did most our learning from the television, seeing as we never went to school down in the Bayou, all we ever did was the cooking and the cleaning and any other chore Momma Syracuse had for us to do. Aunt Gine was a nurse and she worked nights, during the day she would help us learn reading and writing, we couldn't go to school she said because we were too far behind the other kids and didn't want us teased. A couple of years went by and things started getting bad, I guess things got worse than we thought because she started using dope. I don't know why but she did. Everything changed, we had to move from that apartment, she lost her job and then one day she came home and put me out. She said that I was a man now and that I was supposed to be working and making it on my own, I was 12. Gine started hooking to pay for her habit. Dominique told me that Gine shouldn't be alone so she would stay, I don't think Nique wanted to be alone anymore with no one to love her. Gine let her stay but I had to go.

After Zuco and Bear fought, Zuco took off. Bear told me not to worry that he would always be there for us and that he'd never leave. He left a few nights later to go and make some money and didn't come back. Baby and Ep were feeling really bad about everything that was going on and I didn't know what else to do but panic, I pulled myself together and went out to look for Bear and Zuco to talk some sense into those two. Whichever one I found first would get a good talking to. A couple of days later I ran into a couple of ex-island boys, Chuy and El Jefe, they told me they saw Bear stumble out of an alley in Brooklyn and collapse to the ground, they say he was cut up pretty bad. They called an ambulance to come get Bear. They didn't know if he was alive or dead, Chuy told me to find Zuco and let him know what happened but I told him that Bear and Zuco fought and that he took off and I didn't know where to find him. Jefe said that Zuco was dealing dope for this black cat out in Brooklyn and that I would probably find him there. I didn't like going to Brooklyn alone, it took me a couple of days to muster up the courage to go to Brooklyn. I figured if Bear was dead and Zuco wasn't coming back that I better be finding somewhere else to stay. While contemplating whether or not I was going to Brooklyn by myself or if I was just going to leave altogether, I remembered Aunt Gine and Dominique. The last time I saw Nique was when Zuco and I ran into her on the streets of Brooklyn, I thought this was a sign from God that this was where he wanted me to be. I caught the train and went to the address that Nique gave me; she said that if I ever needed a place to stay, money or food to come by and they would be happy to have me. During that chance meeting, Nique told me that Gine had her hooking to help pay rent and keep food in the house. I felt really bad for my sister but with a limited education what else could she do for money. It's kind of the reason I stayed away from them for so long, I knew that this was how her life was going to wind up and I could not stand to watch my sister sell her body just to eat and keep a roof over her head. I went to the address and Gine told me that Nique had come home a couple of days ago and told her that someone tried to rob their pimp and that she believes he killed the guy, so she sent her to an all girls home to hide out for a few days. Gine gave me the address to the girls' home and said that Nique would love for me to visit, because she really missed me. I missed her as well, plus I wanted to see my sister, to see how she was doing, really to make sure Gine and this pimp hadn't got her hooked on dope.

Gine asked if I wanted to stay the night and keep her company because she didn't like being alone. I stayed because there was nowhere else for me to go. We didn't talk much, just watched t.v. until we both fell asleep on the couch. The following morning I woke up under a blanket with Gine in the kitchen making breakfast, it reminded me of when Nique and I first got to New York. Gine told me to go wash and brush my teeth then I could eat but that I had to hurry because Guapo would be coming soon and he didn't like other males in his house. She made rice, scrambled eggs, and toast and sausage patties. I ate a bowl of rice then made a sandwich out of the rest of breakfast and got out of there. Aunt Gine gave me a few dollars and she started to tear up, I closed the door behind me and I heard her crying, I know that this is not how she wanted her life let alone ours. I went to the bodega around the corner from her place and got a coke. That sandwich and the coke kept my mind off of the fear until I got to the home for wayward girls. I didn't know how I was going to get in to see Nique, so I tried the direct approach, sometimes that's the best method, it worked. This rather odd looking white lady answered the door and asked who I was there to see, I said Dominique Syracuse, yeah we took that last name, only because Chuckie and his Momma were who we were sent to live with and because we could pass for white and no one would be the wiser, also because Momma Syracuse could get state money to keep care of us. I hated that lady.

The lady at the girls' home asked me to wait in the front parlor and to have a seat, and she would send Dominique down shortly. She replied how she knew that I was related to Dominique, she said that we could have been twins, I guess Nique didn't talk much either.

Once Nique came down I could tell that she was hooked on something, that damned pimp, we started crying at the same time. We stood in the middle of this room crying and hugging for quite a while, we wiped the tears from one another's faces, and then sat down to visit. I asked how she was doing, she said ok she guesses, I then asked how this place was treating her and she answered it was nice and that she felt safe and comfortable there. I told her that she should consider staying and getting clean, she said Gine needed her and that she would miss her. Gine also said Guapo would be looking for her and that if she didn't come back it would be hell to pay and she was really afraid of him, I dropped the subject. I asked Nique about the incident, what happened with her and this pimp Guapo?

She said she was out on the stroll when Guapo picked her up, he drove around the corner then pulled into the alley, and it was dark and smelly, rats running around, bums pissing in the alley. I was scared that I wasn't making enough money for him and that he was going to beat me, like he did a few of his other girls if they came up short or didn't make any money at all. He started stroking my hair telling me how pretty and sexy I was. He said that if it wasn't for Gine I would probably be dead or out here getting raped by these filthy niggers. He says that he would make me his main chick and that I wouldn't have to turn tricks, but Gine is jealous and would kill us both. He said because she was a junkie and it costs to keep her high, which she gave me to him just to keep the dope in her veins and money in his pocket. I was shaking and crying and he just kept stroking my hair and talking, telling me everything was going to be alright, and then he said he wants me to fix him up so I started to unzip his pants and he grabbed me by the hair, yanked my head up and starts screaming 'not in his car!' He starts barking at *how special his car is and that no one, not even*

he would defile his car. He's angry and violent,

tells me to get the fuck out. We got out the car

and he starts kissing and petting the car, it was

a '78 Cadillac Coupe Deville, his pride and joy.

He tells me to go to the back of the car and wait

for him. I did as I was told and he continued to

talk to the car, when he finally came back there,

he asks me to give him his money then pushed

me down on the ground and tells me to finish

fixing him up, he unzips and I start doing what

he tells me. He starts getting into it when this

guy sneaks up behind him and says "give me the

money". He snatches out his blade, spins around

and sticks the guy. I start screaming and I push

past Guapo, they fall and I see the man that

Guapo stabs is just a little kid, this chubby faced

dark-skinned kid. I thought he slit this kids'
throat, it was so much blood, and this kid was
staring at me like he couldn't believe this was
happening.

I stopped Nique as she was describing this kid; I asked her where this happened. It couldn't be I thought to myself. She told me where and I thought, *Oh my God*! She asked me what was going on so I told her that I knew the kid, he was an Island boy, Bear. She asked if he was a friend, I told her that he was the little brother of Zuco, the kid I was with that day I ran into her on the street. She said that she thought I was dealing because she had seen that guy around a lot selling for a friend of Guapo's. I could not understand why Zuco was selling dope or what Bear was doing here in Brooklyn. Was he looking for Zuco? Why was he in that alley? I told her that she needed to stay here until I can figure out what to do. She said she'd think about it, but she was scared of Guapo. I asked if she knew where Zuco posted up. She told me she would usually see him around a grocery store a couple blocks from Aunt Gine's, mostly at night, she said she was sorry about Bear. I was thinking about how I was going to break the news to Zuco. The lady who asked me to wait in the parlor came back and asked if I wanted any refreshments. I accepted just so I could spend as much time with Nique as possible. When I left I was confused, angry and sad. I lost a good friend and had to tell his brother he was killed and how he was killed or maybe not, I don't know, either way I had to catch up to Zuco and let him know. I waited until evening and went back to Aunt Gine's place to see if I could stay one more night, then I could look for Zuco and tell him what happened. Gine was scared, she looked as if she had been smacked around, and I asked if she was alright. She said she was fine as she tried to hide the bruises on her face. She hurried me in and said that this is the last night I could stay. I asked if he beat her because I was here last night. She said no, that he was looking for Nique and was mad because I knew where she was and refused to tell him so he started hitting me. She locked the door and asked how Nique was. I said scared but I didn't tell her that I knew the guy Guapo stabbed. I just wanted something to eat and a warm place to sleep. The next morning, I got up and fixed Gine breakfast, she was still sleep-I guess sleeping off the beating she took.

After breakfast I got out of there, took a couple of bucks out of her purse because I knew that I would have to post up until night to find Zuco. I went to a playground nearby and hung out there feeding the pigeons and thinking. I got something to eat and waited until nightfall. When you're out just waiting and thinking, time moves very slow. I walked around the area Nique told me about for hours. As it got closer to 11 o'clock, things seemed to go at light speed. I had to act like I knew where I was going and what I was doing because it would look very suspicious of me to just be walking around without purpose. I came up on this group of guys just standing around jaw-jacking and that's when I saw Zuco running across the street to join them. I didn't want to walk back over to these guys and have them question why I was in their space so I waited until Zuco was alone or at least it wasn't so many of them. It was an another hour or so when he walked my way, he motioned for me to come over, he said that he saw me walking up the block and when he crossed the street, he was glad that I didn't approach him at that point or ask the other guys if they knew of him. He asked what I wanted and said that he didn't really want to talk about Bear. I didn't know how to, Zuco said just spit it out. That's when all my thoughts and words started running together, I told him a pimp named Guapo stabbed Bear and that he might be dead and my sister saw the whole deal go down and that Natine and Jefe found Bear on the street unconscious and bleeding and called the ambulance, then the ambulance came and got Bear, but no one knew if he was alive or dead. They didn't even know what hospital he was taken to. I told him it happened a few days ago a couple of blocks from here. Zuco looked as if he zoned out like Jefe used to. I could tell he was high or drunk maybe even both. He started grumbling to himself cussing and hitting his self in the head, and then he just took off. With nowhere to go, I headed toward the subway, hopped the turnstile and headed back home. On the train ride back I couldn't help but think how fucked up our lives must be. What can we do? This is how we live and no one is coming to change things. When I got back to the

spot Baby and Ep were gone. I just flopped
down and cried, didn't feel like going back out
to look for anyone else and wind up finding
more heartache or trouble. I just sat there with
my head in my hands trying to figure this all out.
Damn.

Cover created by Lynette L. Galloway

www.ingramcontent.com/pod-product-compliance
Lightning Source LLC
Chambersburg PA
CBHW030147200626
46812CB00015B/1728